...ainst
...bout
...got
...first

...club trilogy, Jake, Toby, Ravi, Ruth and Nancy form a club to stand up to the bullies (Dave, Ivan and Trevor).

Ravi, Jake, Ruth, Nancy and Toby

Trevor

Dave

Ivan

Spoiler Alert

At the end of the book, Trevor leaves Dave's gang to join the FAB club and help them build their new clubhouse on the lake. This is where we join them for the second book in the trilogy, *FAB Club 2 - Friends Against Cyberbullying*.

FAB CLUB:

Ruth Wilkinson:
When she isn't with the FAB club, climbing trees or riding her bike, Ruth likes drawing.

Nancy Wong:
Nancy doesn't mind being known as a teacher's pet and loves studying, especially computers.

Toby Wilson:
Toby is the smallest member of FAB. When he's home alone, he likes making amazing buildings with his Lego.

Jake Blake:
Jake has his own style and doesn't care about fashion or what other people think.

Ravi Gupta:
Ravi loves reading and works hard at school. Unlike Nancy, he tries not to draw attention to himself. He wishes everyone would play by the rules.

Trevor Skudder:
Trevor is big and strong, but doesn't like to fight. He used to be in Dave's gang, with Ivan.
He loves cooking.

3

AND:

Ivan Carter:
Ivan used to be in Dave's gang and is jealous of the FAB Club, even though he wouldn't want to join it.

Dave Howard:
Dave doesn't have a gang any more and regrets some of the things that happened when he did.

FAB CLUB 2

FRIENDS AGAINST CYBERBULLYING

BY ALEX HALLATT

MOONTOON PUBLISHING

FAB Club
(members only)

Thank you to everyone who has helped in the making of this book. Particularly Izzie, William, Steph, Louis, Emma, Zoey, Jen, Ciadh, Fiona, Carolyn, Sheila, Dale, Duncan, Debbie, Lemon and Jane.

Thanks also to Sheila Glasbey for editing the book before illustration. Remaining errors are my own; email me@alexhallatt.com if you spot any!

CHAPTERS

CHAPTER ONE

A FAB SUMMER

It was the long summer holidays and the FAB club met every day at their new clubhouse on the lake. If it was dry, they usually played games like 50-50 block home, or French cricket. If it was wet, they stayed inside and read comics, books and magazines, or played games.

They took turns to bring lunch. Most of them would bring sandwiches made by their parents, but Trevor enjoyed making the meals himself. Sausage rolls, felafel and salad pittas, carrots, celery and corn chips with three types of dips, and all sorts of other things he had read in cookbooks or seen online.

Some days he got up early and baked. He made muffins, flapjacks, sticky cinnamon swirls, custard-filled doughnuts. One day, he even made chocolate éclairs. Ruth said they were the best things she had ever eaten. Trevor blushed bright red and didn't make them again, because he was afraid they would never be as good. Trevor loved cooking. The only thing he liked more was hanging out with his friends at the clubhouse.

The members of the FAB club were never bored. They put their phones in their pockets, or on the shelf by the door. What they were doing in the FAB club was usually more interesting than whatever was on their phones. Sometimes the phones would beep, but they tried to ignore them, unless it was getting close to home time.

Except for Toby. He was always on his phone, even whilst they were playing cards. Toby put down his cards and fished in his pocket.

"Ignore it, Toby," said Jake. "It's your turn."

"It's a message from Mum. I have to answer it, otherwise she will call me." Toby tapped away on the screen.

"Come on, Toby. It's your go," said Jake.

The phone beeped. Toby tapped. The phone beeped again. Toby tapped.

"This is driving me crazy!" Jake slammed down his cards, grabbed Toby's phone and replied to Toby's mum's texts.

Mum: Hello, darling!
Toby: Hello, Mumsie-poo.
Mum: How are you?
Toby: I'm just splendid.
Mum: What are you doing?
Toby: Losing a game.
Mum: Don't be late for dinner.

Then Jake wrote:

And sent it.

Toby grabbed the phone back. "What did you write? Aaargh! She's going to kill me, you doofus!"

"You shouldn't have done that," said Ravi.

"He shouldn't be spending so much time looking at his phone," said Jake, looking back at his cards.

Toby tapped away furiously on the phone.

Toby put the phone down and glared at Jake.

Toby: Sorry, Mum.
That wasn't me.
Mum: I hope not!
Toby: See you later.
Mum: Okay. Xxxxxxx
Toby: Xxx

Jake grinned as Toby looked back at his cards. He put down a seven. "Pick up seven, unless you've got a seven."

"Ha!" said Jake. "Finally!" He put down three sevens. "Pick up another seven and another seven and another seven and I'm out!"

"Not again!" said Ruth. "You have all the luck, Jake."

"Hey, the rain's stopped," said Ravi. "Let's go out in the boat and see if we can catch any fish."

The FAB didn't have any fishing rods, but they had jam jars on strings. They moulded the bread from their sandwiches into balls and squished them into the bottom of the jars to take out on the boat.

They usually caught minnows and threw them all back. This time, something else came up in Toby's jam jar.

"It's a crayfish," said Ruth, tipping it out on the prow of the boat. "It's a crustacean, like a crab."

"Ugh," said Jake, "it's ugly. Throw it back."

"Let's keep it as a pet," said Toby.

"It's cruel to keep things cooped up," said Trevor, "and crayfish taste delicious when you cook them."

"That's even crueller," said Nancy.

"But you eat other animals," said Ravi.

"Cut it out, you lot," said Ruth. "While you've been arguing, the crayfish has escaped."

"It wouldn't have made a good meal for the six of us anyway," said Trevor. "Let's go and get fish and chips for lunch."

One day in late summer the FAB club were playing "Monotony".

"You can't put all the money from property sales into the middle," said Ravi.

"Why not?" asked Jake, who had just bought Dorchester South. "Yes! I've got all the stations."

"Because the rules say the money has to go to the bank," said Ravi, shaking the box lid.

"But it's more fun this way," said Trevor.

"And quicker," said Ruth.

"Otherwise we'll never finish," said Nancy, rolling the dice. "Double six!" She moved her little cat in a flash and landed on the cinema. "Yes! All that money is mine!" She scooped up

the pile of notes in the middle of the board and the faces of the others fell.

"We'll never win now. Not with all the apartment blocks she's got in Elwood and Carnegie," said Toby.

Ravi threw down the lid and got up from the floor. He went outside and slammed the door.

"I'd better go after him," said Toby, getting to his feet.

"I guess you won again, Nance," said Jake. "I'll see you guys tomorrow." He ran out of the clubhouse and caught up with Ravi and Toby to walk home.

"Winner packs up," said Ruth. She and Trevor headed out.

They hopped from one log to another through the marsh and entered the woodland.

"Which path, Ruth?" asked Trevor.

"Let's take the chestnut walk."

They walked through some fallen leaves. "It'll soon be time to play conkers," said Ruth.

"It's soon time to go back to school, but I don't want to. I've had the best summer of my life," said Trevor, kicking the leaves away.

"Don't worry, Trevor. The FAB Club will be there. We're friends forever, wherever." Ruth put her arm around Trevor as they emerged from the woods. She looked at him and saw his smile vanish. She turned around to see Ivan standing in the middle of the path, grinning his mean little smile.

CHAPTER TWO

GONE FOR BROKE

"Hello, lovebirds," said Ivan.

"We're not lovebirds, we're friends," said Ruth. "But you don't know the meaning of the word, do you, Ivan?"

"Ha, some friend Trevor was, snitching on me to the police."

"Sorry, Ivan," said Trevor, looking down at his shoes. "But we shouldn't have stolen all that stuff. I had to help people get it back from Dave's dad."

"Yeah, because you're such a goody two shoes," said Ivan, as he kicked dirt over Trevor's trainers.

"Cut it out, pipsqueak," said Ruth.

Ivan glared at her and balled his fists, but Trevor stepped between them. "What are you doing here, Ivan?" he asked.

"None of your business."

"Are you following us?" asked Ruth.

"Why would I?"

"You tell us," she said.

"You think I'm looking for your new playhouse, don't you?" said Ivan, jabbing a bony little finger in Trevor's belly.

Trevor stepped back as Ruth stepped forward.

"If you try to burn down this clubhouse, we'll call the police," said Ruth.

"Ha! I don't care about your smelly old tree

house. You don't have to worry about that."

"Good," said Ruth.

Ivan smirked. "Yeah, I'm not going to destroy that," he said, and pushed past Trevor.

Trevor and Ruth carried on along the path to the town. Once Ivan was out of earshot, Trevor turned to Ruth. "He's up to something."

"Don't worry, Trevor. Our club is safe. He's got no idea about the lake house." Ruth climbed over the stile into the lane. "But there is one thing you should worry about."

"What?"

"I'm going to beat you to my gate again!" And Ruth ran down the track.

"Hey! You had a head start! That's not fair!" yelled Trevor as he ran after her, knowing he had lost already.

The next day, in the lake house, Ruth and Trevor told the others what had happened with Ivan.

"I saw him at the bottom of the field a couple of weeks ago," said Jake.

"I saw him at the corner shop this week and he gave me the creepiest smile," said Nancy, with a shiver.

"Do you think he is trying to follow us?" asked Jake.

"That's why I said we should use different ways to get here," said Ravi.

"And we do," said Nancy, as they heard a knock on the door. "We're very careful about that."

Ruth let Toby in.

"Unlike the passwords," said Ravi. "It's only me who asks for the passwords. This week's was 'snotgoblin', in case you've forgotten."

"What use is a password, if Ivan is right at the door?" asked Jake.

"Yes, he didn't need a password to burn down the tree house," said Trevor.

"Never mind Ivan," said Toby. "Did you guys see the letter?"

"What letter?" asked Ruth, looking around.

The rest of the club looked blank.

Toby took an envelope out of his pocket and gave it to her. "My mum got this this morning."

Ruth took the letter out of the envelope and read it.

Dear Parent or Guardian,

Due to unforeseen circumstances, Marypuddle School will not be opening this term.
We apologise for any inconvenience caused.

Yours faithfully,

Mrs Caning

Mrs Caning
Head Teacher

"That's fantastic!" said Jake. "No school!"

"We can keep on meeting at the lake house," said Trevor.

"I don't have to do any homework," said Ruth.

"Haven't you done any homework?" asked Ravi. "My parents made me finish mine ages ago."

"Well, now we can relax. This summer is never going to end!" said Toby, smiling from ear to ear.

All but one of the FAB club hugged and hi-fived over the letter. Only Nancy looked unhappy.

Nearly every Marypuddle pupil was delighted. Most of their parents were not.

There was an outcry in the local paper. An investigation by the reporter, Rebecca Noseypants, revealed more. She interviewed teachers and found that school would not be

starting because there was no money to pay them.
She talked to a blabbermouth bank manager who
revealed how big the problem was.

The school owed the bank exactly one million pounds.

Everyone in the town was shocked, especially the FAB Club. They were in the clubhouse on a rainy afternoon, playing another marathon game of Monotony, when they heard about the million pound debt.

"I can't believe it," said Jake.

"What did they spend a million pounds on?" asked Ravi, as he used £200 to buy Trinity Street.

"I hope it was the canteen. The school lunches were the worst," said Nancy, grimacing.

"Blacknet Catering provides them," said Ravi. "They quoted twice as much as Dad's company, but they still got the contract."

"Well, they don't spend the money on the food. It tasted disgusting," said Jake.

Toby said, "My mum made me sandwiches after the second time I had food poisoning."

"The school didn't spend money on the buildings. They looked as run down as always, when I cycled past yesterday," said Ruth.

There was a knock on the door.

"What's the password?" asked Ravi.

"Pustule," said Trevor's voice from outside.

Ruth unlocked the door and let Trevor in. His eyes looked red and puffy, as if he'd been crying.

"Are you okay, Trevor?" she said.

"Fine. I'm just a bit thirsty," he said, and went to get a glass of blackcurrant squash.

Toby continued, "Who cares what they spent the money on? At least we won't have to go back to school."

"You think our parents are going to let us stay here until Christmas?" said Trevor. "My dad's sending me to Shiverworth School for Boys!"

"That's terrible, Trevor," said Ruth.

"Uh-oh... I wonder what will happen to the rest of us," said Toby.

"We'd better find out," said Jake, as they packed up the game and headed out of the clubhouse.

CHAPTER THREE

NANCY GOES AWOL

When the FAB club met the next day, the mood was grim.

Ravi said, "I asked my parents what would happen to me now that Marypuddle was closed. They said I would have to stay home –"

"Lucky you!" said Toby.

"– to be home-schooled," continued Ravi.

"Dad says he'll take time off from his company to teach me. He said that I would be able to study twice as hard for twice as long."

"Ouch," said Jake.

Toby sighed. "I wish I could stay at home. I have to go to boarding school like Trevor."

"Cool! You're coming to Shiverworth?" said Trevor.

"No, I'm going to Croakington," said Toby, looking nearly as sad as Trevor did.

"Flippin' heck. Are none of us in the same school?" said Ruth. "Mum's sending me across town to Granite Towers School. What about you, Jake? Are you going to Granite Towers?"

"No. Mum is sending me to stay with Auntie Joan in Dumchester," said Jake. "She said there's a good school there. She wouldn't send me to Granite Towers."

"Isn't Granite Towers any good?" asked Ruth, looking worried.

Jake paused, then said, "It's bottom of the league table."

"Well, there has to be one school at the bottom. Maybe all the schools are good," said Ravi, putting an arm around Ruth's shoulder.

"I wouldn't mind where we went, if we were all in the same school," said Ruth, blinking away a tear.

"Don't worry, Ruthie," said Jake. "We can all keep in contact with our phones. We'll get Nancy to top them up with our membership money before school starts. Then we can send each other plenty of messages."

"Yes! A virtual FAB club," said Ravi.

"Where is Nancy?" asked Trevor.

"She hasn't messaged us," said Toby, looking at his phone.

"Let's message her now," said Ravi, and the rest of them got out their phones and logged into PicPoke.

Where are you?

At home.

 Why?

I've got something important to work on.

 More important than FAB club?

If I don't sort this out, we're all going to be separated.

 What school are you going to?

Marypuddle School for Young Ladies ☹

 Young ladies?
Are you sure they'll let you in? ☺

Ha ha. Gotta go.

Toby's phone beeped.

Mum: Your pizza is getting cold.

"Oops! Dinnertime! I'd better go," he said.

"Crikey, I didn't realise it was that late," said Ravi. He picked up his backpack and rushed out of the door. "Don't forget to lock up!"

The others locked up the clubhouse and went home for their dinners.

"See you tomorrow!" shouted Ruth.

"My turn to bring lunch!" replied Jake.

"Great," said Trevor. "I love those spicy, peanutty salad wraps." He felt hungry at the thought of them.

Nancy didn't come to the clubhouse the next day. Or the day after that. Or the next week. When the FAB club messaged her, she said she was busy. Then she sent a message saying:

Don't message me any more. I'll be back.

Any more messages were unanswered after that.

Ruth was heading out to the lake one sunny Saturday and went into the corner shop to buy a bottle of squash. She nearly bumped into Nancy, coming out with a big packet of crisps.

"Hey, Nancy! Good to see you."

"Hey, Ruth. How's the club?"

"Great, but we miss you. What have you been up to?"

"I've been doing some research. On the school's finances."

"Oh, I see," said Ruth. "Why didn't you tell us? We've been messaging you and when I called you it kept going to your voicemail."

"Sorry about that. You can't trust the network. Whoever did this has been able to hack into systems people thought were secure."

"Whoever did what? What systems?"

"Look, I've got to go. I'm nearly done. I'll explain everything at the club."

"Cool. So we'll see you soon?"

"Yes, but don't tell anyone this until I get there."

"Okay, Nancy. Take care of yourself."

"You too, Ruth," said Nancy, and she was gone.

CHAPTER FOUR

THE LAST LUNCH

On the last day of summer holidays, Ravi was the first to arrive at the clubhouse. He turned the combination lock to 5707 and it sprang open.

He opened the door, went inside, shut the door and slid the bolt across. Each member of the club said the password before Ravi let them in.

"Bum," said Ruth.

"Bum," said Jake.
"Bum," said Toby.
"Bum," said Trevor.

They were playing dominoes and Ravi was losing badly, when there was a knock on the door.

Ravi leapt up to put his hand on the bolt.
"What's the password?"
"Bottom," said the voice on the other side.
Ravi didn't move.

"That's Nancy," said Toby.

"We haven't seen her in ages," said Trevor.

"Come on, Ravi, let her in," said Jake.

"She has to say the password," said Ravi.

Everyone in the clubhouse was laughing, except for Ravi.

"She's messing with you, Ravi," said Ruth.

"Let her in," said Jake.

"Rules are rules," said Ravi and folded his arms as he leaned against the door. There was a long pause.

Finally, Nancy shouted, "BUM!" as loud as she could.

Toby slid the bolt and let her in. "How are you doing, Nancy?" he said.

"Where have you been?" asked Jake.

"I've been doing some school work…"

"What? I thought you would have finished your homework in the first week," said Ravi.

"I did," said Nancy. "I've been working on the problem the school has. It took me a while, but I got into their bank account and it's a mess."

"No kidding," said Jake. "That's why they had to shut down."

"Yes, but a month ago they had plenty of money. They had £255,000."

"Woah, that is a lot of money," said Trevor.

"Yes, but three weeks ago it started to disappear. It disappeared 99 pence at a time. Nobody notices when 99p disappears, and the system they had didn't need approval for 99p withdrawals."

"99p isn't much," said Ruth.

"It is when it's being withdrawn every second for just over two weeks."

Ravi scribbled some calculations down on a notepad.

Woah!

0.99×60 (seconds)

$=$

$\times 60$ (minutes)

$=$

$\times 24$ (hours)

$=$

$\times 14$ (days)

$=$

"Why didn't the bank stop them taking out more money? That's always happening to Mum," said Ruth.

"Yes, and it would have happened normally, but this little hacker took care of that. Before he drew out the money, he changed the agreed overdraft limit from £5000 to a million pounds. After nearly fifteen days, they were a million quid overdrawn and the bank stopped any more withdrawals."

"Where did all the money go?" asked Ravi.

"That's what I'm trying to find out," said Nancy. "But I'm tired of working on this. I thought I'd come and join you for lunch. Whose turn is it?"

"Mine," said Trevor.

"Awesome," said Nancy, and Trevor beamed as he unpacked his backpack.

There was a choice of noodle salad with sesame beef strips, or halloumi and courgette fritter wraps with a sweet chilli sauce. Trevor had also made millionaire's shortbread and apple and vanilla custard turnovers for dessert.

"This is a bit spicy," said Nancy, chewing on half a wrap. Trevor looked crestfallen.

"But I really like it," she said, as he reached for the other half.

"This salad is delicious," said Jake.

"It must have taken you hours to make all this," said Toby.

"I was up pretty late last night," said Trevor, yawning. "But I really enjoy doing it. The time flies by."

"This lunch is the best I've ever tasted," said Ruth.

"You always say that," said Trevor.

"That's because your cooking gets better and better, Trev," said Jake.

"It sort of feels like the last meal a prisoner gets when they are on Death Row," said Ravi, wiping caramel from his chin.

Everybody stopped talking.

"Way to go to bring us down, Rav," said Ruth.

"It's not the end of the club. We can still chat online," said Jake.

"Yes, but we need to be careful," said Nancy, digging into her backpack. She gave them all envelopes. "These are new SIM cards. Put them in your phones when you want to contact the FAB club. The numbers of everyone here are written on the inside of your envelopes. Don't give these numbers to anyone outside the club. Don't trust anything you read from anyone else."

"Even my mum?" asked Toby.

"Especially your mum," said Jake, giving Toby a nudge.

"Blimey, Nancy. Is all this techno-spy stuff really necessary?" said Ravi.

"Yes," said Trevor, who was starting to look a bit tearful.

"What's wrong, Trevor?" asked Ruth, putting her arm around him.

Trevor put his hands to his eyes to hide the tears. Everyone else looked at each other, puzzled. Trevor didn't say anything, but swiped open his phone and handed it to Ruth.

"Oh, Trevor..." she said as she read the messages. She passed the phone around for the FAB club to read.

"You know that's nonsense, don't you, Trevor?" said Ravi.

Trevor looked up and nodded a little.

"Yes," said Jake, "we like you AND your cakes."

Trevor smiled.

"Who are the messages from?" asked Toby.

"They are anonymous," said Nancy, "but I bet they're from someone who knows your phone number. That's why we should all change them."

"I'm changing mine now," said Trevor, as he removed his old SIM and threw it in the bin.

Everyone else put in their new SIMs and numbers and sent some messages to test the system.

The FAB club were going their separate ways, but only in the real world.

CHAPTER FIVE

BOARDING SCHOOL BLUES

Trevor's dad drove him to Shiverworth School for Boys on the Saturday before term started.

"Why can't I stay home until Monday?" said Trevor, as his dad lifted his bag out of the boot.

"I want you to have a chance to settle in, lad."

"But I could make roast lamb tonight and we could have shepherd's pie tomorrow."

Trevor's dad thought about the food for a moment and then closed the boot. "That's a lovely offer, Trevor, but I'll get a takeaway curry tonight and go down to the club tomorrow. They do roasts on a Sunday." He hefted the bag onto his shoulder and walked up the steps.

Trevor trudged behind him. "Their Yorkshire puddings are as tough as old boots. And their gravy is lumpy and –"

"True," interrupted his dad, "but I'll have to put up with it." He reached the doors to the school and put down the bag. "Now, work hard and see if you can get onto that rugby team, eh?" Trevor's dad gave him a slap on the back and trotted back down the steps to the car, without looking around.

Trevor watched him drive off, picked up his bag and went through the doors. He followed the signs for new arrivals and an older boy behind a desk gave him a thick folder about the school. It contained a lot of history, a big list of classes and an even longer list of rules.

RULES

1. No running, or jumping, in the school buildings (except the gymnasium).

2. No talking in lessons without permission.

3. No shouting, spitting, or swearing.

4. No long hair and no shaven heads.

 5. No uniform alterations, badges, or patches.

6. No leaving the school grounds without permission.

7. No animals to be brought onto the school grounds.

8. No noise to be made after 8.30 pm, or before 6 am.

9. No food to be eaten outside the dining hall.

10. All dining hall food must be eaten.

 11. No phones to be used, except between 6 pm and 6.30 pm on Sundays.

12. No phone calls to be made to non-family members.

"These aren't nearly as fun as the FAB club rules," thought Trevor. He sighed and found his way to his dorm.

Trevor's boarding school was a big change from Marypuddle. It was weird, not going home after classes, eating every meal in silence in a vast dining room and having to sleep in a big dormitory with dozens of other boys. He had been put in with the other new students, who were all much younger than him. On the Monday, he had to wear school uniform for the first time. He had no idea how to tie his tie and needed to ask one of the kids in his dorm how to do it. He heard the boy and his friends giggling about it later. The blood went to Trevor's face and he felt like the tie was strangling him.

Hee hee hee

When Trevor went into his first class, he scanned the room to see if there was anyone he knew, but saw a sea of unfamiliar faces.

Until he reached the back row. There was Dave Howard.

He'd had a haircut, but it was unmistakably Dave. Trevor's heart sank, but then Dave gave him a weak smile and a nod of recognition.

Trevor nodded back, but was careful to sit a few desks away from him. He didn't want to become part of Dave's gang again. He would keep out of his way and hope Dave kept out of his.

Trevor hated being at boarding school. After the classes for the day ended, he would walk out through the playing fields to the edge of the school grounds. There was a massive brick wall that ran around them. It was twice as high as he was, but there was a section where steel pegs had been hammered in, nearly to the top. He was able to climb up and look over. He gazed out over the green fields and wished he could fly above them and be at the lake house.

As well as the FAB club, Trevor missed being able to cook. He was only able to cook once a week, in cookery class. They made boring things like cabbage soup, tapioca pudding and meatloaf. Even that horrible food tasted better than what they served up in the dining hall. It was the same menu every week.

 **MENU**

Monday:
Porridge ❋ Mutton Surprise ❋ Lentil & Turnip Bake

Tuesday:
Porridge ❋ Lentil Surprise ❋ Liver & Onions

Wednesday:
Porridge ❋ Liver Surprise ❋ Swede & Kidney Pie

Thursday:
Porridge ❋ Kidney Surprise ❋ Tripe & Brussel Sprouts

Friday:
Porridge ❋ Tripe Surprise ❋ Bony Fish Stew

Saturday:
Porridge ❋ Fish Surprise
❋ Sardine & Mustard Mess on Toast

Sunday:
Porridge ❋ Roast Mutton & Twice-Boiled Vegetables
❋ Mutton Soup

Trevor wanted to message the FAB club every day, but that was against the rules. Shiverworth boys were only allowed thirty minutes to be on their phones, at 6 o'clock on a Sunday afternoon. He was supposed to use it to talk to his dad, but his conversations with him were over in five minutes. The rugby was on at 6 o'clock and his dad didn't like to miss too much of it. Trevor didn't mind. It gave him twenty-five minutes to catch up with his friends and find out how things were in their schools. He discovered that his school wasn't the worst.

CHAPTER SIX

LOOK WHO'S HERE

Granite Towers was a big school in a tiny piece of land, surrounded by factories. There were no trees, or grass, or anything green, except for an occasional weed poking up through the cracks in the crumbling playground. When you went through the rusty school gates, there were crumbling stone steps that led up to the doors to the school. Going through them, it took a while for your eyes to adjust to the gloom. The corridors were lined with dark wooden boards and smelled like the contents of an antique shop that sold things no one wanted. The classrooms weren't much better, as it seemed like every window looked out onto a brick wall.

Ruth gritted her teeth and went to her first class. It was History. Ruth usually found that listening to history teachers sent her to sleep. When she opened the classroom door, she was overwhelmed by the noise. Kids were yelling and screaming, or laughing at stuff on their phones. She couldn't wait to see what happened when the teacher turned up. But then she saw the teacher. He was in the corner by the window, with his back to everyone. He was typing into his phone, mostly ignoring the class.

When a badly aimed ball of paper hit the back of his head, he turned around and shouted, "Cut that out, class; cut that out!"

There was silence for a few seconds. Then giggles. Then full-on laughter, and the yelling and screaming started up again as the teacher turned back to his phone.

"I guess I won't be falling asleep in this class," Ruth thought.

It was the same in every class. The kids were

running riot and the teachers were giving up. Ruth gave up going to the classes too. She took her textbooks to the library and taught herself. She found that she had lots of time left to draw, and sent pictures of the crazy goings-on at the school to the rest of the FAB club.

Kevin brought an eel into English class because he says it ate his homework. BURP!

Sandra played the spoons in Spanish class and no one else noticed. chk? chk? chk!

Martin won the biggest bubble gum bubble in Biology, but it burst all over his face.

Ruth thought that Granite Towers wasn't going to be so bad, after all. But then she received a nasty shock. One lunchtime, she was running down the stairs from the library and bumped into a boy coming up them. The boy pushed back the hood that was over his hat and swore. He looked up to see Ruth, who had frozen on the step above.

It was Ivan. She took a moment to recognise him, because he wasn't wearing the same old clothes from before. He was dressed like a little hip-hop rapper. He was wearing a baseball cap and several layers of clothing that looked way too big for him. On his feet was a pair of trainers that were crazy white. He was decked out in chains around his neck, a big gold bracelet and a chunky gold watch.

Ivan scowled at Ruth and then pulled a gold phone from his pocket. He punched the screen a few times and hissed, "You're going down, loser," under his breath. Then he hopped around Ruth and carried on up to the library at the top of the tower.

After that, Ivan kept his distance from Ruth. Other kids weren't so lucky. He would threaten little kids by their lockers, or trip them up in the corridors. If Ruth approached him, he'd shrug

his shoulders, give her his mean little smile and
pretend that nothing had happened.

One day, Ruth looked up the stairs and saw
Ivan push a girl at the top. She fell down the first
flight of stairs, but Ruth caught the girl before
she could fall any further.

"I saw that," said Ruth to the girl, who was shaken and speechless. "Let's go and tell someone."

The girl shook her head, grabbed her bag and ran off.

Ruth told a teacher what happened, and the teacher said she would keep an eye on Ivan. Ivan seemed to behave better, for a while. Then Ruth noticed that the kids with phones would often be standing over them, crying. When she signed into PicPoke, she saw Ivan was writing nasty things about them or posting horrible photos online.

Ivan picked on one kid in particular – Quentin Tipton. He was always yelling at him, or twisting his ear, or pinching his arm. Quentin was a shy boy and taller than Ivan, but skinny as a shoelace. He spent most of his time in the library, but he was never reading. He was always tapping away on his laptop. Whenever Ruth walked towards him, he snapped the laptop shut and blinked up at her, nervously.

Ruth missed the rest of the FAB Club. Her heart lifted every time she got a message from them. Sunday afternoons were the best because everyone was online. She told them about Ivan and there was a flurry of messages in response:

Oh no. 😕

 Ugh. Ivan turns up when you least want to see him.

 Which is always.

Yes, he's like a that you try to flush away but keeps bobbing back up in the bowl.

 LOLS

 Seriously, Ruth, be careful.

 Don't worry. He's keeping out of my way. He knows I have the FAB club. He can't do anything to me now.

Don't be so sure. He's smarter than you think.
Take care, Ruth - I have to go.

 Me too.

Bye, everyone. I miss you guys.

CHAPTER SEVEN

PICPOKING ON TOBY

Croakington was much smaller than Trevor's boarding school. Toby's dorm had six beds and the boys he shared with were all younger than him. The boys often asked Toby for help with their homework and Toby didn't mind giving it. He wasn't used to people looking up to him and it made him feel good. He felt like their older brother.

Sometimes he joined in their games, especially if they were playing with Lego. They combined

all their sets so that they had thousands of bricks and were able to make giant fairgrounds, castles and spaceports.

There were fewer than twenty pupils in each class. When Toby was struggling with a problem, he only had to look up and the teacher would come over and help him. He began to understand a lot more of his Maths lessons.

His grades were the best they had ever been, and his mum was delighted. They talked on the phone every evening and she sent him lots of texts to say how proud she was of him.

Toby used his new SIM every Sunday to join in on the FAB club chat. The rest of the time he had to use his old number, so that his mother could contact him. The others knew this and messaged him from their old numbers too.

Mum: Toby, do you have enough clean pants, or should I send more?

Toby: Have you been talking to Jake?

Mum: No, darling. He's in Dumchester. Why? What's happened?

Toby: Nothing. Just wondered. I have enough underwear, thanks.

Toby: Gotta go, Mum. I have homework to do.

Mum: Good boy. I love you xxx

Toby: Love you too. X

Toby switched back to PicPoke, but Jake and Ruth weren't online. Instead, he saw a distorted photo of himself. When he clicked on the avatar of the sender, the name came up as "Friend" and there were no other details.

Toby didn't reply, and another picture popped up.

Aren't you reading? Don't worry. I'll post these to the public PicPoke page. Then everyone can see them.

"Friend" went offline. Toby switched to the Croakington page and saw the pictures appear at the top. He tried to delete them but couldn't. He clicked "hide these posts" and they disappeared.

But everyone else could see the pictures. When he passed by some girls near the water fountain, they pointed at him and giggled. One of them started to suck her thumb. Toby felt upset.

"What's the matter, Toby? They're just silly pictures," said one of the girls.

"Yes, don't be a baby," said another, and the three of them collapsed in laughter.

Toby walked away, his eyes pricking with tears.

Later that evening, Toby's phone rang. It was his mum. Toby answered the phone and told her about his day. He didn't tell her about the pictures, but he saw that the boys in his dorm were looking over and smirking. When he finished the call they asked him if he'd like to play Lego.

"I'm too old to play that," he said, but watched them enviously as he waited for the BuzzBlatt game to launch on his phone.

He started playing, taking his bees through the first few levels. He gathered pollen and nectar and built his hive. When his bees were fully loaded, he entered the Killing Fields. He got thousands of points, zapping the people carrying big cans of pesticide. Toby was about to advance to the Industrial Complex level, when his phone vibrated. A squadron of planes appeared out of nowhere. Chemical spray covered his swarm. His bees were dead. Game Over.

A screen flashed up.

Toby clicked "cancel". A new screen asked, "Are you SURE?"

Toby clicked "cancel" again and the leader board came up. He had 111,969 points and was second on the board. Only Tallboy was ahead, with 420,666 points. "I bet he's allowed to buy credits," thought Toby, as he exited the game.

A message popped up on PicPoke. It was another picture of him, this time in a big pile of cow dung. The caption read "Loser".

Toby switched off his phone.

CHAPTER EIGHT

OFFLINE AND ON

When the FAB club had their PicPoke Sunday meeting, Toby told the others about the pictures.

It's probably Ivan.
He sends nasty messages to everyone.

Yes, he's trying to upset us. I get messages from a "Friend" on my old number and ignore them.

So do I. He must have all our old numbers.

But some of the things he says are true.

Toby was glad they couldn't see him crying.

Cheer up, Tobe.
We're your real friends. You
can ignore the fake ones.

But he's right about my ears.
And other things.

You don't have to be perfect,
you know.

Yes, that's Ravi's job.
LOL.

Someone has to do it.

Switch off your phone. I haven't
had any bad messages since I
started the new term.

That's because you're never
online, Trevor.

Trevor's right. Every time our
phones are on, there's a chance
someone can hack into them.

Nancy's paranoid, but if you can't ignore it you should turn off your phone, Toby.

I can't. Mum would kill me if she couldn't contact me.

Maybe you should tell her you're being bullied.

Maybe. Hey, thanks everyone. I feel better now. 👍 😊 👋

When Toby put his old SIM back in the phone, he had six texts from his mum and a stream of PicPokes from "Friend".

They showed his head on a donkey, his face pasted onto a monkey's body, and him coming out of a giant nose, like a bogey. Then Friend's avatar flashed up on the screen.

Hey, squirt, I've been trying to talk to u.

Toby ignored him.

 Can't u heer me with those big ears of yurs?

 Is it becoz yur talking to mummy?

Toby closed PicPoke and swiped open his texts.

Mum: Hello, sweetheart.
Mum: Where are you? x
Mum: Are you doing homework? xx
Mum: Do you need anything? xxx
Mum: Hello?
Mum: HELLO?

Toby called her back. "Hi, Mum."
"Oh, there you are. I was getting worried."

"I'm fine, Mum."

"Are you sure, sweetheart?"

"I'm okay."

"You don't sound okay. What's wrong?"

Toby broke down and told her about the bullying messages.

"That's awful, Toby, just awful! Don't worry, my little boy. I'm going to sort that out right away, you hear?"

"Yes, Mum," said Toby. "I love you."

"I love you too. See you soon."

Term had another four weeks to go. Before Toby could ask what she meant, she rang off.

The next day, Toby was called into the headmistress's office. His mum was sitting in one of the chairs in front of the desk. They both had cups of tea and there was an empty plate on the desk.

Mrs Holme motioned to him to sit down. "Hello, Toby. I understand you've been receiving some nasty messages on your phone."

Toby looked at his mum, who nodded. "Yes, miss," he said.

Mrs Holme held out her hand. "Please may I see them?"

Toby opened the photo gallery on his phone

and gave it to her. She looked at them, expressionless, before placing the phone on her desk. Toby's mum picked it up and scrolled through the pictures with wide eyes.

"Do you know who sent you these, Toby?" asked the headmistress, leaning forward over her desk.

"Not really. I think it's a boy in another school."

Mrs Holme relaxed. "Ah, well. If you do find out, let me know and I'll follow this up, okay?" She smiled at Toby's mum.

"That's it?" said Toby's mum. "You aren't going to do anything?"

"There's not much we can do, Mrs Wilson.

Not unless we know who sent those messages."

"Hrrmph!" said Toby's mum, throwing the phone in her bag as she stood up. "Well, they won't be messaging you any more, sweetheart." She gave Toby a big hug and a sloppy kiss. "Look after yourself, darling, and we'll see you at the end of term." She flounced out of the door, closing it behind her with a bang.

Toby looked bereft.

"Don't worry, Toby," said Mrs Holme. "You can use my phone if you need to call your mum. Now run along back to your class."

Toby moped through the corridor. "How am I going to contact the FAB club now?" he thought.

Jake didn't mind Dumchester School. It wasn't so different to Marypuddle, except for not knowing anyone there. He kept himself to himself and listened to his music during the breaks. It wasn't so bad.

What was bad was his aunt's cooking. She said that she was experimenting with fusion cuisine. Jake didn't know what that was, but he did know that fish bone dumplings with wasabi guacamole, sweet and sour bolognaise, curried eggs and liver pie were revolting. Jake wasn't the only one to turn his nose up at Auntie Joan's food. When Joan's back was turned, her boyfriend, Nate, gave most of his plate to the dog. Jake did the same, and Biggles got fatter and fatter.

Fortunately, on Sundays Nate insisted on cooking roast dinner and Jake enjoyed a good meal before chatting with his friends.

When Jake signed into the PicPoke group five minutes late one Sunday it was only him and Trevor.

Ravi was on the phone to Nancy. She had called him ten minutes before.

"I'm on to something, Ravi. I've found the hacker who drained the school's finances."

"Brilliant! Who is it?"

"QTip."

"That's not a real name, Nancy."

"I know it's not. That's the problem. I need to find who QTip really is. I've been following his digital footprints, but once he goes into the dark web, I lose him."

"You've lost me too."

"Everything you do on the normal internet can be monitored by anyone, right?"

"Right... I guess... Really? Everything?"

"Yes, really, Ravi," said Nancy. "Unless you use a part of the internet called the dark web."

"Uh-huh," said Ravi, who was still thinking about everything he had done on the internet being seen by anyone.

"The problem is that the money from the school disappeared into the dark web. I can't track where it went without the help of QTip."

"Maybe we can help you find QTip," said Ravi.

"No, not yet. I have to keep this under wraps. Anyway, I'd better go. Say hi to everyone."

CHAPTER NINE

THIS SPELLS TROUBLE

When Nancy rang off, Ravi quickly signed in for the PicPoke FAB group chat. Jake and Trevor were chatting about school lunches.

Dumchester's are better than Marypuddle's canteen lunches.

That's not saying much.

I miss your lunches, Trevor.

😁 Don't we all?

😃 Hey, Rav! Where are Toby and Nancy?

I don't know about Toby, but I just got off the phone to Nancy.

I knew you would have a reason to be late.

She says she's made a break through. Something about a hacker called QTip.

Oops.

What?

I wasn't supposed to tell you yet.

Don't worry, Ravi. Nancy is paranoid.

Where's Ruth?

 She was online. It looks like she just logged off. She didn't say much anyway.

Maybe something is bothering her. I saw her online yesterday, but when I called her it went straight to voicemail.

 Hey, she's back on. Hello, Ruth.

Hi. Wot duz Nancy no about QTip?

I don't know.

How are you, Ruth?

Better than u lot. LOL.

Ruth's avatar went offline.

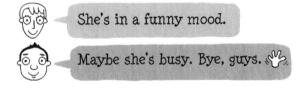

She's in a funny mood.

Maybe she's busy. Bye, guys.

The boys all signed off.

Ravi didn't like being home-schooled. He had to have lessons from after breakfast until five o'clock in the evening. They only had a short break for lunch, when his dad usually microwaved leftovers from the night before.

At five o'clock, he was supposed to go to his room to do his homework. That's when he turned on his phone and checked for messages from the rest of the FAB club.

At first the messages had been the highlight of the day. He loved finding out what his friends had been doing, or seeing Ruth's funny drawings, but now it seemed that everything had changed. In the last couple of weeks, everyone but Ruth had disappeared.

Hi, Ravi. Wots happening?

Nothing much.
No one else is online.

 U haven't herd anyfink?

No. What's with your spelling?

 Nufink. We can't all be
teechers pets like u.

Yeah. Dad would go mad if I
didn't spell things correctly.

 I bet he doesn't get
as mad as mine.

What do you mean? Your dad
left when you were little.
Has he come back?

 U fink you r so clever. U don't
no nufink. U just a dork.

Really?
Well you are being mean.

Ruth's avatar went offline. Ravi tried to call the rest of the club, but only got through to their voicemails. Ruth was being horrible, but what about the others? Why weren't they talking to him? It wasn't his fault he was clever.

Ravi turned off his phone, as his dad called up the stairs, "How's that homework going?"

"Er... it's really hard, Dad," he said as he opened his books.

His dad popped his head around the door. "Good. You need a challenge, son."

"Yes, Dad."

"If you're going to be a successful businessman like me, you'll have to work hard."

"Okay, Dad," said Ravi. "I'd better read this chapter one more time and try again."

"That's the spirit," said his dad as he closed the door.

Trevor turned on his phone on Sunday. The only person online was Ruth.

How r u?

OK. School is the same old rubbish. And Dave keeps trying to talk to me.

 Dave? Wich Dave?

Dave Dave. Dave Howard.

 Wot does he want? He isn't talking to me.

I don't know and I don't care. Hey, where are the others?

 They sed the club is over.

What? Really?

 Yeh. Wots the point? We can't meet. We r in difrent skools. No one is mesedging any more. It is OVER. FAB club is ded.

No, it can't be.
I ♡ the FAB club.

Trevor's eyes blurred with tears and he switched off the phone. He threw it in his bedside locker and mashed his head into his pillow. He punched the mattress and muttered, "Stupid, stupid! STUPID!"

He only stopped telling himself off when someone poked his back.

"Trevor? Are you okay?"

Trevor lifted his head, turned and looked up.

Dave Howard was standing over his bed.

CHAPTER TEN

PHONEY PHONE FRIENDS

Ruth was becoming worried. After the first few weeks of messaging with the rest of the FAB club, it all went quiet. When she messaged them on PicPoke, no one replied. When she called them, she could only speak to their voicemail. Then she started to get the messages.

We don't fink u look rite.

What do you mean?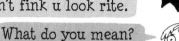

 Your clothes r all 2nd hand.
U r always wearing trowsers.
Old, smelly trowsers.

Mum says there is nothing
    wrong with second hand.

 U look like a boy.

 Yeh.
Why don't u grow your hair?

 Is it coz u have nits?
U gave us all nits.

And a
picture
of Ruth
flashed
up with
bugs
running
all over
her head.

I don't have nits.

 And another fink -

But Ruth quit out of PicPoke. She shut down her phone and scratched her head. Maybe she did have nits. But why would the rest of the club be so mean to her? Everyone gets nits. She went downstairs and talked to her mum, who got out the nit comb.

"Clean as a whistle," she said afterwards. "Why did you think you had nits?"

"Some friends have them," she said. "Well, not friends, exactly. People I know." Ruth blinked a tear away and went upstairs so that her mum wouldn't see her crying.

Meanwhile, Dave asked Trevor, "Are you okay?"

"Go away, Dave."

"I have something to tell you. Something about Ivan."

Trevor turned over and frowned. "I'm not in your gang anymore, Dave."

"I know that. I don't have a gang. But you have the FAB club, right?"

"I don't know." Trevor swung his legs over the side of the bed, sat up and scrunched his fists in his eyes.

"What's wrong, Trev?"

Trevor looked down at his hands. "I'm not supposed to talk about FAB club outside of FAB club."

Dave waited.

"But it looks like it's falling apart," said Trevor, looking up at Dave.

"That's what he wants you to think. That's what he wants to happen."

"Who?"

"Ivan."

"How do you know?"

"He's been calling me to boast. He likes to show off when he thinks he's winning. He told me he found a way to get to Ruth."

"What's he done to Ruth?" said Trevor, standing up.

"Nothing physical," said Dave, stepping back. "But he got close to her one day and cloned her phone."

Trevor's eyes widened. "Ivan copied Ruth's phone onto his?"

"Yes. With the help of a hacker friend."

"If he had control of her phone, he could pretend to be her."

"Exactly."

"No wonder she's been so weird."

"And he had access to all her contacts."

"The FAB club."

"He said he had enough information for his hacker friend to do some real damage."

"Is his friend called QTip?"

"I don't know, but he said the kid was working for him now."

"Yeah, that makes sense. He couldn't do all this on his own." Trevor thumped his pillow. "What a weasel!"

"What are you going to do, Trev?"

"I need to tell Ruth."

"But you can't call her."

"I know," said Trevor. He got out his notepad and began to write.

Two days later, Ruth found a letter addressed to her:

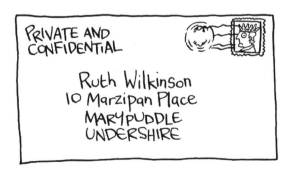

She read Trevor's letter as she munched her cereal. She nearly spat out her Cheerybyes when she came to the part about how Ivan had cloned her phone. "Ivan! Of course. The little poohead." She folded the letter away in the envelope and put it in her pocket. "And Quentin is his hacker friend."

Ruth yelled goodbye to her mum, grabbed her backpack and ran out of the door. She ran to Granite Towers, through the gates and up the stairs to the library. She found Quentin tapping away at his laptop in the corner.

He closed the laptop and looked up at Ruth, waiting for her as she got her breath back.

"Hello, Quentin," said Ruth. "Or should I call you QTip?"

CHAPTER ELEVEN

PENPALS

"How do you know about QTip?" said Quentin, looking worried.

"We know a lot about you and Ivan," said Ruth.

"But how? I was anonymous. There was no trace, no way to find me."

"You should know that anyone can be found on the internet, Quentin. You only need a clue or two, and the help of a few friends."

"Ivan says he's my friend and I have to be loyal to him. Or else."

"Quentin, he's not a real friend if he's threatening you."

Quentin went silent.

"Why did you help him hack us, Quentin?"

Quentin sighed and told Ruth how it started. Ivan had climbed a tree next to his house and used his phone to film Quentin doing a dance to an Andy Armarda song. Quentin didn't

know Ivan was there until he showed him the video. He said he was going to post it to PicPokeTV, so that everyone could see how good a dancer he was.

"Are you a good dancer, Quentin?" asked Ruth.

"No. I looked stupid. Especially since you couldn't hear any music on the video clip."

"Then what happened?"

"Ivan said he wouldn't post it if I helped him with one thing. He said it would be just one thing."

"What thing?"

"He told me that he'd been bullied at his last school, by a kid called Trevor. He wanted to get his own back."

"Ha! That's not true."

"He showed me a photo of Trevor. He's a lot bigger than him."

"But Trevor wouldn't hurt a fly," said Ruth. "Unlike Ivan."

"I know that now, but I didn't know it when we were sending messages to Trevor's phone."

"So, why didn't you stop helping Ivan?"

"He said that now I'd bullied Trevor, he had more dirt on me. He was going to tell Trevor and everyone on PicPoke that I was the one sending the messages."

"That sounds like Ivan."

"He made me hack into the school bank account. I told him I couldn't transfer any money, even if I wanted to. We could look, but not touch."

"But over a million pounds was taken. Somebody touched it!"

"Not me. Ivan used someone else's code on my laptop to drain the money."

"Where did he get the code?"

Quentin paused. "I can't tell you."

"Quentin, you hacked my phone, you sent me nasty messages. You owe me."

"I helped Ivan clone your phone, but it was him who sent the messages. It wasn't me."

"Okay, but why couldn't you tell someone?"

"Ivan used my laptop for other stuff. He said I should be careful, in case my online identity was sent to the police 'accidentally'. It was my digital footprint. No one would believe that Ivan was behind all the hacking."

"What other stuff?" asked Ruth.

Quentin looked worried. "Nothing. I shouldn't have told you anything."

The bell rang for the start of school.

"I'd better go," said Quentin, and leapt up from the desk.

"Let's talk later, okay?" said Ruth, getting up to follow him out of the door. But Quentin had vanished.

Ruth looked for Quentin at morning break, but couldn't find him. He was nowhere to be seen at lunchtime either. After school ended, Ruth walked home and thought about what to do next. "I bet Ravi would know what to do," she thought to herself. "Or Nancy, or Trevor, or Jake, or even Toby." She needed to talk to the rest of the FAB club. Except she couldn't; not by phone.

She stopped at the corner store and bought a book of first class stamps. When she got home, she dashed upstairs.

Her mum yelled up, "Hello, honey! Fancy a cup of tea?"

"In a minute, Mum. Um... I've got some homework to do."

"Well, that makes a change." She waited for a reply, but didn't get one. "I'll bring your tea up."

Ruth's mum knocked on the bedroom door. She went in and found Ruth writing away at her desk. "I'll leave the tea and biscuits here," she said, closing the door quietly behind her as she left.

Ruth was still writing when her mum brought up a plate of lasagne and peas. She wolfed down her dinner and then finished the letters. She wrote the same thing to Trevor, Nancy, Ravi, Jake and Toby. Her hand was aching by the time she had finished. She couldn't believe people did this all the time before phones.

In the first part of the letter, she told them about her conversation with Quentin. She finished the letter with this:

I'm not sure I can trust Quentin. He is very afraid of Ivan. I don't know what we should do next. We need to talk and figure this out. Let's meet on Sunday at six, like we used to. Not on our phones – we can't trust our phones! But let's meet for real, at the club-house. I know it may be difficult for you to get there, but this is <u>important</u>.

See you on Sunday,

Ruth x x x

Ruth posted the letters that evening and waited.

CHAPTER TWELVE

ESCAPE PLANS

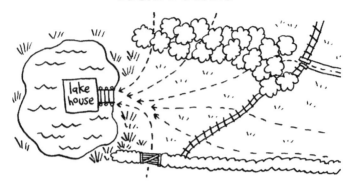

Nothing came in the post the next day. Or the next. But on Friday morning she had a reply from Ravi:

Dear Ruth,

I'm so glad to hear from you. And to see that you can still spell words properly.

See you on Sunday.

Yours sincerely,

Ravi

On Saturday morning, Toby, Trevor and Jake's letters arrived:

Dear Ruth,
Great to hear from you. My mum took my phone away so I couldn't contact anyone. I didn't think about writing letters. Duh!
Anyway, I'll slip out on Sunday and see you then.
Lots of love from TOBY xox

Good plan, Ruth. Now I have to make My own plan to escape the guards (ha. ha).
Trevor xxx

Hello Stinks!

Just kidding. I was worried about you, Ruth. I should have known that Ivan was behind all this. Don't worry—we'll sort him out. Somehow. I think Nancy has found out a few things that can help us. We'll talk on Sunday. I've persuaded Auntie Joan to visit her sister (my mum!) on Sunday. I called Mum and she invited her for a late lunch. We're going to stay over so that they can open a bottle of wine. They won't miss me when I go to the club!

See you soon. Jake xxx

Only Nancy hadn't replied. Maybe her letter was in the post.

Nancy found it easy to fit into Marypuddle School for Young Ladies. She made sure her uniform was spotless. Her skirt was exactly the right length. Her shirt was always tucked in and her tie was tied perfectly. She paid attention in class, got the highest marks in her homework and impressed all the teachers with her hard work. The books she took out from the library were meant for children much older than herself. When she asked if she could use the computers at the library for extra study, nobody objected. Nancy used every break time to get online and follow the trail of the hacker. She brought in soup for lunch and drank it through a straw as she worked.

Each Friday, she gave her mum her class results.

"Straight As! That's wonderful, darling," she said every time. "We'll have to find a way to reward all that hard work, won't we?"

"I guess so," said Nancy.

After Nancy tracked the school bank account break-in to QTip, she thought she had solved it. He had created a back door to the account with a sweet piece of code. That back door let her in too. She only had to follow the money and see what bank account it ended up in. But there was more code in the way and it wasn't as easy to break as QTip's. Somebody else was involved.

It took weeks for Nancy to break the code before she could follow the digital footprints. They led her to the edge of the dark web and a person called Tallboy. But that was as far as she could get. Tallboy had a key to unlock part of the dark web that Nancy couldn't access. She needed that dark-key. She needed to find Tallboy.

She was thinking about the dark-key the following Saturday at dinner, when her mum dropped an envelope on the table.

"Oh, by the way, this came for you."

Nancy recognised Ruth's handwriting. She sliced open the envelope with her butter knife. "Why didn't you give this to me earlier?"

"You were so busy working; I didn't want to disturb you, darling."

"It's from Ruth," said Nancy. "She wants to meet up at the clubhouse tomorrow."

"But we're going to your Auntie Karen's birthday lunch."

"Which Auntie Karen?"

"The one on your dad's side."

"Oh. That one," said Nancy. "Mum, you said you wanted to reward me for all my hard work. I want to meet with my friends."

"Okay, darling, but you'd better ask your father," her mum said as her dad looked up from his plate.

"What's that? Ask me what?"

Nancy told her dad about the letter.

"That's fine with me," he said. "If I could get out of going to that lunch, I would too."

Her mum shot him a look and went back to eating. Her dad gave her a wink and Nancy smiled.

CHAPTER THIRTEEN

FAB CLUB MEET

Nancy got to the lake early, unlocked the clubhouse and went inside. She re-read the letter as she put a new SIM in her phone and started it up. Then she sent Quentin a message.

Hi, Quentin. I'm Ruth's friend, Nancy. We need to chat.

I can't. PicPoke isn't secure.

I know. But you're on Hacknet, aren't you?

Yes.

I'll send you a private message there.

Nancy closed PicPoke and logged into Hacknet.

HACKNAN: HELLO, QTIP.
QTIP: OMG, YOU'RE HACKNAN?
I LOVE YOUR WORK.
HACKNAN: THANKS. WE WANT TO HELP YOU.
QTIP: OKAY. HOW?
HACKNAN: YOU NEED TO GIVE ME TALLBOY'S DARK-KEY.
QTIP: I DON'T KNOW WHO YOU ARE TALKING ABOUT. AND I DON'T HAVE THE DARK-KEY. I'VE GOT TO GO.

There was a knock at the door and Nancy glanced up. When she looked back at her screen, QTip was gone.

"Darn it," she said. She signed off and shut down the phone.

There was another knock at the door.

"Come in, it's open," said Nancy.

"Fiddlefarts!"

"Ravi, it's only you who knows the password. Come in!"

Ravi came in and gave her a big hug.

One by one, the others reached the clubhouse.

"I'm amazed you could all get here," Ruth said.

"Only just," said Trevor. "When I made my way to the school gates, they were locked."

"What did you do?" asked Toby.

"I climbed over the wall, but it was a long drop on the other side. I landed badly and I think I sprained my ankle. It really hurt to walk here from the bus stop."

Ravi reached for the box of membership money. "Hands up if you think Trevor should call a taxi to take him back."

Everybody's hands shot up.

"Thanks, guys," said Trevor.

"Don't thank me," said Toby. "Croakington's on the way to Shiverworth School. The taxi can drop me off too."

"Okay," said Ruth. "We'd better get to business –"

"Yes," interrupted Nancy. "But not here. I don't know that it's safe."

"Yes, the room could be bugged," said Jake, making his eyes go wide.

"There are lots of bugs," said Toby, watching a beetle scuttle across the floor.

"No, seriously guys, someone could be listening in," whispered Nancy. She put her phone on the table and motioned for everyone else to do the same.

Then they followed her outside and got into the rowing boat.

Once they had rowed out into the middle of the lake, Nancy relaxed and started to speak. She told them what she had found about the money that had gone from the school; how it had disappeared into the dark web.

"I've been trying to get more information from Quentin, but he's been avoiding me," said Ruth.

"I was messaging him before you arrived," said Nancy.

"Great, can he help?" asked Ravi.

"Not much. He says he knows nothing about Tallboy."

"Tallboy?" asked Trevor.

"The person who has the dark-key to get into the dark web," said Nancy.

"Tallboy's the one who always beats me on BuzzBlatt. He's top of the leader board by miles," said Toby.

"That's Ivan," said Trevor. "Ivan is 'Tallboy' on BuzzBlatt. He loves that game."

"You guys still play BuzzBlatt?" asked Nancy.

"Yes," said Toby, "don't you?"

"I used to, when I was little, but it became too easy," said Nancy. She took her other phone out of her pocket.

"Hey, why are you allowed to have a phone and we're not?" said Ravi.

"I've encrypted it." Nancy launched BuzzBlatt and scanned through the users. "Darn it. Tallboy isn't online. We're going to have to do this later."

"Do what, Nancy?" asked Jake.

"Set a little trap for Ivan. We'll see how much he loves BuzzBlatt when the whole FAB club are playing."

"What do you mean?" asked Ruth.

"I need to crack the code and Quentin can help me. Ruth, try and talk to him again. If he's scared of Ivan, we need to reassure him." Then Nancy gave them all new SIMs. "You can put these in your phones when we get back to the clubhouse. But try not to use them until you get a message from me."

"How will we know it's from you?" asked Ruth.

"Good point," said Nancy, and frowned.

"How about you use a password?" said Ravi. "If you send just the word 'GetShorty', we'll know it's you."

"Ravi, for once, that's a great idea," said Nancy, and Ravi grinned.

Ruth went to school early the next day and found Quentin in the library. He looked like he was expecting her.

"Hacknan, I mean Nancy, sent me a message. She says you have a plan to sort this all out," said Quentin.

"Yes, but we need your help."

"Okay, but I need to tell you the rest of what happened first."

"Shoot."

"Ivan got the code to take the school's money from an online message board. Something called Buzzblam, I think."

"BuzzBlatt, it's a game."

"That's it, yes. I think computer games are a waste of time, but Ivan's always playing them."

"I used to play BuzzBlatt, before I joined the FAB club. It's a good game."

"Yes, well, Ivan said someone from BuzzBlatt would help him. As well as the code, they were going to give him extra BuzzBlatt credits and pay him some real money. Five percent of the total we took from the school."

"Why didn't Ivan take the lot?"

"Because any computer nerd could trace it. But they offered to clean the money via the dark web. Then they paid it into his bank account."

"Five percent of all that money is a lot," said Ruth. "Ivan stole a lot of money. You should have told someone then."

"Yes, I wish I had, because then it got worse."

"How?"

"They offered Ivan a key to the dark web."

"The dark-key."

"Yes. The dark-key gave Ivan a way to get more credits for BuzzBlatt and share in the game's profits."

"What profits?"

"Ivan takes all the money kids pay for game extras. He pays ten percent of that to a dark web company called Blacknet."

"That's a deal. Is that all they wanted?"

"To begin with, but now Ivan says they want weird stuff."

"What stuff?"

"I don't know and I don't want to know. That's why I need to stop this. You have to help me stop this." Quentin was looking really worried.

"We will," said Ruth. "Nancy thinks you can help her fix all this."

"Really?" Quentin brightened. "How?"

"She'll message us when she's ready. The code word is 'GetShorty'."

Quentin giggled.

CHAPTER FOURTEEN

THE STING

At 5:06 pm, on the Thursday before term ended, Nancy sent a text to Quentin and the FAB club's phones.

Ruth, Jake, Ravi and Quentin were ready and waiting.

GetShorty

Trevor's phone vibrated and he went to the loo for some privacy.

Toby was in the school garden. He made sure no one was watching as he went behind the shed.

They all texted back.

Nancy: Ivan's on BuzzBlatt and we need to keep him there. FAB – start playing and don't stop until I text you 'GotShorty'.

The rest of the FAB club launched BuzzBlatt and began to play.

Nancy: Quentin, I'm sending you code to break into the back end of the game. Distract Ivan with some visuals. I'll start helping the others. We need to make him mad.

Quentin: That shouldn't be hard.

He found Tallboy's avatar and made some changes.

Toby: Tallboy looks hilarious. And he's lost control of his bees – I've got them.

Nancy: You're not doing very well, Ruth.

Ruth: I haven't played this for ages!

Nancy: How about we give you another swarm too?

Nancy tapped out some code and Ruth saw her swarm double in size. With a little help from Nancy and Quentin, the FAB club took their swarms through the next levels until they reached the top level of the game. Then Nancy typed in some lines of code for Tallboy.

--

Ivan was furious. What on Earth was going on with his avatar? And his score was terrible. The FAB club were beating him on BuzzBlatt. But he'd show them. He just had to use his credits to buy a massive swarm. Then they would see who were the losers.

Ivan clicked on the 'buy swarm' button. A screen popped up.

TOP SECRET

YOU HAVE 0 CREDITS

"What?" shouted Ivan, and bashed the phone with his fist. Another screen popped up.

ENTER DARK KEY TO GET 1000 CREDITS

KEY: ☐ – ☐ – ☐ – ☐

"Ha!" Ivan tapped in the key and was back in the game.

GotShorty

They didn't need to keep playing, but the FAB club continued until they ran out of credits. Tallboy thought he had won.

132

--

HACKNAN:
WE'VE GOT IT, Q!
QTIP: YES!
I'M FOLLOWING
TALLBOY'S DIGITAL
FOOTPRINTS NOW.
WATCH THIS.

Quentin shared his screen with Nancy's laptop.

QTIP: THEY TAKE US TO A COMPANY CALLED BLACKNET.

ENTER YOUR DARK KEY

HACKNAN: OKAY, HERE GOES... WE'RE IN!

QTIP: YES, BUT LOOK AT THAT DIGITAL VAULT. HOW DO YOU BREAK INTO THAT?

HACKNAN: I'M ON IT.

Her fingers were a blur as Nancy typed streams and streams of code.

QTIP: WOAH! NOW WE'RE REALLY IN!

HACKNAN: LOOK AT ALL THAT CASH!

QTIP: OVER 20 MILLION BITCOINS! DO YOU KNOW HOW MUCH THAT IS IN REAL MONEY?

HACKNAN: A LOT. BUT LET'S FIND THE REAL MONEY. IT WILL MAKE THE TRANSFER EASIER.

QTIP: THERE'S AN ACCOUNT HERE WITH £2,411,956 IN IT.

HACKNAN: THAT WILL DO. NOW TO MOVE SOME OF THAT BACK TO MARYPUDDLE SCHOOL...

Nancy transferred the money to an account she had set up earlier. And then another account. And another.

HACKNAN: CAN YOU GET INTO THE SCHOOL'S BANK ACCOUNT?

QTIP: I'M IN. WOW – AND SO IS £1,255,000.

HACKNAN: LET'S ADD AN EXTRA MILLION, TO COVER EXPENSES.

QTIP: IT'S IN. GOOD WORK. TIME TO CLOSE THE HOLE. I'M CORRUPTING THE CODE. DONE.

HACKNAN: WHAT DOES THAT LEAVE US?

QTIP: £156,956.

HACKNAN: DARN IT. I CAN'T ACCESS THE GUDGAMEZ-2-PLAY ACCOUNTS OF THE KIDS WHO PLAY BUZZBLATT.

QTIP: WAIT A MO. I CAN. NOW WHAT?

HACKNAN: I'M DIVIDING THE REST OF THE MONEY BETWEEN THEM. THEY SHOULD ALL HAVE PLENTY OF CREDIT NOW.

LET'S GET OUT AND CORRUPT THE DARK-KEY BEFORE WE DELETE ALL TALLBOY'S ONLINE DATA.

QTIP: WAIT! WE CAN'T LEAVE THE BITCOINS THERE. THOSE GUYS ARE BAD PEOPLE. THEY

DON'T DESERVE THAT MONEY.

HACKNAN: WHAT DO WE DO WITH IT?

QTIP: I'M LOOKING UP SOMETHING... YES, THEY'LL DO...

And in the blink of an eye, over twenty million bitcoins vanished from the vault – just before Quentin and Nancy did.

On the last day of school, Ivan found Quentin in the library.

"Quentin, you have to help me."

"With what?"

"I can't access anything on the internet. All of my passwords are invalid."

"Oh, that's a shame."

"You'll help me get back in, right?"

"No. I'm done helping you, Ivan."

"What?" Ivan grabbed Quentin by his ear.

"Ow! Let me go!"

"Do as he says," said Ruth, who was standing at the door. She walked towards Ivan and Quentin.

"Who's going to make me?" hissed Ivan. "You can't make me do anything."

"Maybe not. But a company called Blacknet might."

Ivan let go of Quentin. "What do you know about Blacknet?"

"That they've just lost all of their money. And

it was taken by someone with access to their dark-key. Someone called Tallboy. They're looking to wipe him out online... or the person he really is."

Ivan went white. He muttered something rude, turned off his phone and ran out of the library.

"Nancy and I deleted all his online data," said Quentin. "Blacknet have no way of knowing who Tallboy was."

"Ivan doesn't know that. He won't be bothering other kids online for a while."

CHAPTER FIFTEEN

SCHOOL'S GOOD FORTUNE

As the term ended, the head teacher of Marypuddle School sent out a letter:

Dear Parent or Guardian,

The financial error that occurred with our bank account has been corrected.

Marypuddle School will be opening next term.

We look forward to welcoming back your child.

Yours faithfully,

Mrs Caning

Mrs Caning
Head Teacher

The parents of the FAB club were relieved. Toby's mum had missed him. Nancy's parents didn't mind where she went to school, as she always had good grades. Ravi's dad's company wasn't doing as well without him being there. Jake couldn't stay with his aunt forever and Ruth had told her mum the horror stories of what Granite Towers was like. Trevor's dad had found it hard to pay Croakington's school fees and Trevor hadn't been happy there. His dad read Trevor's report card to find that Trevor had run away one Sunday, and was sometimes found hiding in the toilet.

The FAB club enjoyed the Christmas holidays hanging out at the clubhouse. On Boxing Day, they talked about their presents and ate delicious things that Trevor had made with leftovers.

"Being reunited is the best Christmas present I could get," said Toby, and Jake gave him a friendly shove.

"I'm so happy we didn't get any homework," said Ruth.

"I'm glad to eat Trevor's lunches again," said Jake.

"Yes, I'm not looking forward to eating school lunches next week," said Nancy.

"Can't you bring sandwiches?" asked Toby.

"She doesn't have to, and neither do you," said Ravi, winking at Trevor.

Trevor folded his arms with a smile.

"What do you mean?" asked Jake.

"It's a secret. But don't bother bringing sandwiches to school."

At lunchtime on the first day back at school, the FAB club met under the monkey bars.

"I never thought I'd be glad to be back here," said Ruth.

"Yeah, what a dump," said Jake, looking around at the broken swings and the paint peeling off the climbing frame.

"It won't be a dump for much longer," said Nancy. "The school has got an extra million to spend now."

"Won't they have to give that back?" said Toby, looking worried.

"They'll find that difficult. It has been given to them by the Foundation Against Blight."

"Who are they?" asked Ruth.

"A charity that looks after people who can't look after themselves. The money comes from anonymous donors," said Nancy, looking at her friends.

Ravi grinned. "Are those the same anonymous donors who gave over one hundred thousand million pounds to the Society for the Betterment of Children?"

"The very same," said Nancy.

"Hey, where's Trevor?" said Ruth.

"He's at the canteen," said Ravi. "Let's go and see him."

"Ugh," said Jake. "I wish I had brought sandwiches. You didn't tell me we'd be having lunch at the school canteen."

"Blacknet aren't the contractors anymore. They went bankrupt," said Ravi, looking at Nancy.

"I wonder how that happened...?" said Jake, as he looked at Nancy too.

Nancy smiled. "It seems that there was an enormous hole in their finances."

"My stomach feels like it has an enormous hole in it," said Toby. "Can we go and eat lunch?"

The FAB club went to the canteen, grabbed trays and lined up to be served.

Ruth looked around at the tables. "Where's Trevor?"

"Right here," said Trevor. He was standing behind the counter, wearing a catering uniform.

"What are you doing there?" asked Toby.

Ravi explained, "When Blacknet went under, the school asked companies to bid for the catering contract again. I told Dad that Trevor was brilliant at making lunches."

Trevor continued, "His dad called me and asked if I could come up with some menu plans."

"And he did," said Ravi. "Dad used the plans in his bid and his company won the contract."

"His dad is employing me as a consultant," said Trevor, pushing his shoulders back with pride.

"Are you being paid?" asked Nancy.

"Not exactly. Not with money, anyway..."

"Then how?" asked Jake.

"FAB club members get free lunches," said Ravi, smiling at Trevor.

"Awesome!" said Toby, helping himself to a

slice of mozzarella, tomato and basil pizza and a side salad.

The rest of them loaded up their trays and Trevor joined them at one of the tables.

"This lunch is the best I've ever tasted," said Ruth.

"Hear, hear!" agreed the others.

Trevor grinned from ear to ear.

Hey - thank you for reading!

That's all from the FAB Club for now. If you enjoyed reading it, please leave me a review. It will help me write the next book about the FAB Club.

My author page:
amazon.com/author/hallatt
Or look for me on GoodReads.

Cheers!

Alex

Alex
alexhallatt.com

GLOSSARY

(WHAT WORDS MEAN)

You probably know a lot of these words, or think that everyone knows them, but sometimes words are different in England, Australia, New Zealand, the USA, Canada, India and other places where they speak English. This book is written in English English.

Avatar – an image representing someone.
AWOL – Absent WithOut Leave. An old army term that means disappearing without telling anyone (or getting permission).
Badge - I think you call these "buttons"

in America.

Bereft – sad because you don't have something.

Billion – American billions (a thousand million) are smaller than English billions (a million million).

Bin – trash can.

Bogey – booger, snot.

Boot – trunk of a car.

Courgette – zucchini.

Crisps – potato chips. England has the best flavours of crisps. Bacon, prawn cocktail, roast chicken, cheese & onion, and salt & vinegar were what I liked growing up. But now there are even more flavours.

Doughnut – donut. We English like to spell things with more letters.

Encrypted – information and communications are hidden using code.

Holiday – vacation, or time off. The summer holidays usually last at least six weeks in England.

Pants – underwear, undies, briefs,

knickers, smalls, tighty-whities, grunders. Not trousers.

Post – mail.

Shop – store.

SIM – a card that stores the phone number and other data on a mobile (cell) phone. It stands for Subscriber Identification Module, which means nothing to me.

Snitching – telling on someone.

Stile – wooden steps to climb over a fence. You usually find them on public footpaths.

Sting – as well as the painful part of something like a bee, this has another meaning in this book. It means when a trap is set by the FAB club to catch Ivan.

Squash – a concentrated drink or cordial. Usually a fruit flavour. Blackcurrant is the best.

Trainers – training shoes, or sneakers.

ALEX HALLATT

Alex Hallatt was born and brought up in the West Country in England. She emigrated to New Zealand, where she met her partner, Duncan, and his dog, Billie. They spent a few years living in Australia, England and Spain and are now back in New Zealand. You can read more about that in her monthly *Illustrated Epistle* (sign up for the newsletter at alexhallatt.com).

Alex was bullied at school, but found her friends and is now happy to be following the first three rules of FAB Club (though she is breaking Rule Number 6 a **lot**).

FAB Club Rules

1. Don't be a bully.
2. Help people who are being bullied.
3. Have fun.
4. Only FAB members are allowed in the clubhouse.
5. Password must be used to enter clubhouse.
6. No-one is to talk about FAB club outside FAB club.

FRIENDS AGAINST BULLYING – JOIN THE CLUB!

Go to alexhallatt.com/fab for bonus stuff (like some of Trevor's recipes and how to play 50-50 block home and French cricket).

One last thing.

If you, or someone you know, has been bullied in real life, you can get help. The following pages give you some advice on what to do. You can also go to these web pages to get more help and advice about bullying:

www.kidscape.org.uk (UK)
www.netsafe.org.nz (New Zealand)
www.kidsline.org.nz (NZ child helpline)
bzaf.org.au (Australia)
www.antibullyingpro.com (UK)
www.stopbullying.gov (USA)
www.violencepreventionworks.org (USA)
www.stopabully.ca (Canada)
bulliesout.com (UK)

IF YOU ARE BEING BULLIED:

1. Tell someone. Talk to an adult you trust - a parent, a teacher, or a family friend.

2. It is not your fault. Don't blame yourself. There is never a good reason to bully other people.

3. Often bullies pick on kids who are different, but being different can be a good thing. If you are not being unkind to other people, you do not deserve other people being unkind to you.

4 You can make yourself less likely to be bullied. If you act confident, people will think you are confident and then you are likely to **become** confident!

Stand up tall, with your shoulders back (not in a crazy way - think of looking like a president and not like a chicken).

Take your time to reply to other kids. Look them in the eye and think of the right thing to say, which might just be "no". It may even be best to say nothing and walk away, or you might want to change the subject. Don't insult people, just show them that you are your own person and will not be bullied.

5. Don't make changes for other people - make them for yourself. Who do you want to be? What do you want to do in your life?

6. Find other interests that are fun for you. Ask an adult, if you want to find a club to join and other people who share your interests. In this way, you might find children who are more like you, who can become your friends.

Remember that friends make you feel good. They may not always agree with you, but they should support you. If you find that spending time with friends always makes you feel worse, it is time to make new friends.

CYBERBULLYING

If you are bullied online, or via your phone:

1. Tell someone. Report the bullying to the website administrator. If it continues, tell an adult you trust.

2. Do not reply to bullying remarks. Use website or app settings to block people who send you messages that upset you.

3. Make any online account private, so that you can only be contacted by friends and not strangers, or people you do not want to contact you.

4. If being online makes you unhappy, **stop**. Being online, or on your phone is not somewhere you have to be, like school. Ignore what other children say you should do, if it is not what you want to do. You are the boss of you.

IF YOU SEE SOMEONE ELSE BEING BULLIED:

1. If you feel safe in the situation, tell the bully that what they are doing isn't cool.

2. Invite the kid who is being bullied to hang out with you for a while.

3. If the problem continues, it is okay to tell a teacher, or an adult you trust.

REMEMBER THE FIRST THREE RULES OF FAB CLUB:

1. Don't be a bully.
2. Help people who are being bullied.
3. Have fun!

More information on FAB Club and bullying is at alexhallatt.com/fab.

And you can always write to me and be one of my friends who are against bullying.
Alex@alexhallatt.com

33435820R00090

Printed in Great Britain
by Amazon